CHRIST
THE LOST YEARS

SIR CHARLIE BROWN

Pharos Books

ISBN: 978-93-91103-06-4
eISBN: 978-81-19094-56-1

©Publisher

Publisher: Pharos Books (P) Ltd.
Plot No.-55, Main Mother Dairy Road
Pandav Nagar, East Delhi-110092
Phone: 011-40395855, +14049995474
WhatsApp: +91 8368220032
E-mail: sales@pharosbooks.in
Website: www.pharosbooks.in
First Edition: 2022

CHRIST—THE LOST YEARS
SIR CHARLIE BROWN

The Bible consists of 66 different books, all written by different authors, at different times, years after the death of Jesus. But what about his childhood? John 21:25 KJV. There are so many books out there about the life of Jesus; but what about his youth? How did he grow up? Was he bullied? Did he have a tree house or a dog? Did he grow up like you or I? What was it like for a boy like Jesus? Because of his abilities, was he picked on in school by other boys his age? Did he have girlfriends?

Basically, this book is fiction for not many things do we know of this little boy who would grow up to be the most talked about man for centuries.

So if you are ready, let's return to the days when camels and mules were the main modes of transportation and begin our story.

1

Two years ago a baby was born. It wasn't the best place to have a baby. The pregnant lady had given no announcement she was coming so the stable hand didn't have time to clean it up. There was poop from the animals, not to mention fur and hair flying about. And due to the smell, all one could do was to hold their nose.

By mid-morning the next day, a man named Joseph and his wife Mary figured it was not the best place in town to raise their baby they called, Jesus. Yes sir ree, Bob, the family had to move. So, After looking about for a house to rent, they found one in the country.

It's been two weeks now, since the time of his birth. The happy occasion continued as folks of the town heard of the unusual birth and came and congratulated the family.

But life stops for no one, and Joseph being a labourer knew the little money he had saved up wouldn't last long. In need of money, Joseph sold his ass on which they rode into Bethlehem. It bought food temporarily, but not for long, he knew he was going to have to get jobs to be able to support the family, after all the new taxes he came to pay took up most of his money.

So, for the next few days, the man looked for odd jobs to build his finances back up.

There were times he hired himself out as a stable boy cleaning out the stables for local people. Then at times, he would pour coffee at different inns. One of the traits he was good at was carpentry. Many would hire him, just for that. He'd fix doors and wooden floors. Mary in the meantime nursed the new baby with what little they had.

As soon as Joseph had some money they quickly moved to a new location away from the odour of the stable.

Stories spread about the family that had a baby in the stable. So, he was special to the townsfolk who had heard of this unusual birthplace. Born in a manger in the stable? News like that travels fast and before you knew it, everyone was talking about it.

The rented place was good for the time being but you had people in the apartment building that were noisy all night long and the rent wasn't cheap either. So Joseph and his wife bought a new mule, packed their stuff on it and headed out of town with the baby. They managed to rent a house in the country.

The house was comfy, with four walls, a roof, and a dirt floor to boot. It was made out of stone but for the moment it would do even though it was chilly inside. On one side of the room, a fireplace had been built and Joseph Immediately went out and chopped firewood. Mary helped bring the wood in and set it in the fireplace.

Using two flints she scraped them together and tiny sparks flew from them and landed on the dead leaves along the logs starting a fire. The heat felt so good.

Mary prepared the family food while Joseph watched the baby.

A mile away from the house flowed a stream of water. Mary would carry her baby and a bucket each day so they would have a cool drink of water in the hot sun. Eventually, Joseph built a cart for her to fetch the water in.

Joseph worked on the house digging a hole far out back this would be used as an outhouse.

Jesus played out in the dirt piles his father created. He was learning to walk by now and when his mother came home with water he would stagger towards her calling out, "Ma-ma."

Of course, he would fall a lot but there always was a hand that would lift him back on his feet again.

The outside was made of stone just like their house had been made of.

The countryside around the house was beautiful with trees and hills and a nearby field where an old farmer use to raise wheat. Alongside there was a forest. Many animals lived there like birds, small animals, and big animals

The little white house in the country was located two miles out of Bethlehem. One time the family witnessed a giant beast crossing the field. The beast was as big as a house. It lumbered along slowly until it disappeared out of sight over the hill.

Mary began to dream, as newlyweds do of what to do with the room in the house. "Over there in the corner, I'll have Joseph build me some shelves next to the fireplace. I'll store pots there so I can boil water in."

Joseph spoke up getting just as excited as his wife. "Here I'll cut a hole for a door to my carpenter's shop."

All the time his parents were planning; Baby Jesus just sucked his thumb.

The days were fun playing with the little baby. His

His favourite game was playing peek-a-boo from under the blanket with his mother who would have a blanket over his head and then remove it quickly. His mother would feed him and then let him play outside in the shade of the house.

Jesus was talking now and saying more words than, "Ma-ma". Before they knew it,

Jesus had grown up to age two and a half years simply playing.

His mother liked the brown curls on top of his head as she watched him play in the sunlight.

He also liked to play with his toys of rocks and pebbles on the ground in front of him, while his father could be heard creating wooden tables and chairs to sell.

Mary was a good cook, taught by her mother and the aroma of his mother's cooking brought in different travellers to join them in eating. It helped to support them in times of need. Sometimes the travellers would pay, other times would leave a trinket of some kind.

In the evening either Joseph or Mary fetched water for the next day so she could go on cooking. In fact this was good for Joseph as well, he would show the journeymen the products he made in his shop, and sometimes he made a sale.

Mary didn't mind going to the stream for water because it was a relaxing time for her as she listened to the birds chirping overhead. While Mary went to fetch water she covered the little food she had with a cloth to prevent flies from getting their portions.

One bright sunny day Joseph heard drums in the distance beating loudly over the horizon. It slowly grew closer to their residence; it got louder the closer it got.

Mary came out and joined her husband to see what was happening. Jesus toddled next to her, saying, "Boom, boom."

"What could that be, Joseph?" Mary asked sounding concerned.

"Sounds like a festival, heading down our road," he replied.

The drumming got louder.

A horseman, trotted by their home and Joseph called out to the rider who was looking in the direction of the sound. He asked, "What's happening?"

"It's a caravan of some sort; with drums and horns and it looks like they are carrying tents on camels."

"Looks like something is going on like a festival or something. What is the caravan for?" Joseph asked.

"I don't know. That's why I'm going to see." With that, the man on the horse lurched forward and galloped off in the direction of the sound.

As Mary and Joseph watched, over the distant hill they began to see the shadows of what appeared to be a parade, heading up their road.

As it drew closer, he made out some of the riders were wearing bright shiny crowns followed by many others walking alongside them all wearing nice robes. No commoner ever wore these kinds of robes. Unless they were a king or festival workers.

"What on Earth was going on?"

The caravan came and stopped in front of their house. One of the kings looked up and saw a bright star pointed at the house of Mary and Joseph.

The king looked at them and in a kingly voice said, "We have come from afar. We followed the star for a very long time and it has finally come to rest above your house."

The two parents turned and looked up as well to see a bright star lingering above their house. Both of Jesus' parents were speechless. Mary ran and grabbed her son and held him. In his own way, the baby was full of smiles and welcomed the strange guests.

An elephant reached out his trunk to touch Jesus but Mary pulled her son closer to her.

The king laughed. "Sorry, ma'am. He is a well-trained elephant we call him Rondo. He just loves to touch babies. RONDO, he demanded put your trunk down."

The elephant obeyed his master's command.

"Forgive us for our intrusion, we were following the Star of David. And it brought us to your house."

"That's funny, that's what the shepherds had said the night our baby was born. They too were following a star and it led them to us. Is that star going to follow us the rest of Jesus' life?"

"Sir I have no idea what God has in store for your baby. But I assure you he is special."

It was at this moment all the kings, wise men, and slaves gathered around Josephs's house.

"We have come to pay homage, to this child. We bring him gifts from distant lands."

"Gifts?" Joseph questioned.

"Yes. In our caravan, we have brought the child GOLD."

About ten or so slaves pulled off some duffle bags, and you can tell they were heavy by the way they carried them.

The king spoke again, "To do a mission, one needs to have money. So, here are many bags of gold for him to use. Mrs. Christ, where shall we put these bags?"

Mary ran to the house ad motioned for the slaves to follow her. They did just that and in the corner of the room placed the bags of gold.

By now the caravan had been followed by a lot of townspeople but the king's security stopped them so they could not see what was going on.

Joseph counted more than ten kings at his doorstep.

Another king stepped up. "Sir, from my land we give thee royal child, the gift of FRANKINCENSE."

With a motion of his hand, one of the servants brought forth boxes filled with FRANKINCENSE.

"This gift is used in our religious ceremonies. When burnt it gives off a fragrance of energy."

A third king took steps with his camel and also motioned to the slaves, who brought golden pots.

And last is rather a strange gift to give a child, but we were told by the spirit what to bring. So now, we present to your child Myrrh,"

"Myrrh!?" Mary replied shocked. "That's used at funerals to embalm a dead body."

"It's also used to tend wombs," the king corrected.

"Isn't that the stuff used in burying folks?" Mary asked.

"Yes, it is."

"Why would you give a baby something like that?"

"Joseph, you are man enough to know your child is very special to this world. These gifts are to represent your son's life, the road he is going to take while we're here on this planet."

Sadly, Joseph nodded his head that he understood.

"Do you have any more children or babies?"

"Not yet. But she is expecting. In a while, we'll soon have another."

Mary then offered these rich folk something to eat. "We don't have much but what we have is yours."

"That's mighty nice of you. We'll go take care of our animals and if it's okay with you, Joseph we'd like to camp here for the night."

"Oh sure. There's plenty of space across the road in that field."

Mary prepared a bunch of biscuits, hot drinks, and potatoes for those men setting up a camp. She noticed she had only three potatoes left. Worried, she went and told Joseph who remarked, we'll give them the rest of our food and a lot of water. It's all we can do."

Mary shook her head in embarrassment.

It was late into the night and the crew and all continued to eat. This puzzled Mary how could three potatoes feed all these men and yet they came back for seconds and thirds?

2

After a night of eating and drinking the wisemen and slaves went to bed with a full stomach. Everyone was breathing softly or snoring. There were three of the kings that did not have a good night's rest.

These kings were having a restless night due to an angel that appeared in their dreams.

The dream began with an out-of-focus hallway, as it went deeper down the hall a figure slowly appeared. It took on the appearance of King Harrod's palace. His face had a false smile on it. It was a big room filled with people dancing and being merry, laughing the night away.

Suddenly King Harrod stood up and motioned for the room to be cleared except for the wise men who came to see this old king. The room was suddenly emptied. There stood the wise men alone with the king.

The king motioned to the men to approach his throne. The dreamers recognized this to be the scene in which they sought out the king for directions, a few years back to find a newborn king about to be born. They lost the star and that is the reason they were here. King Harrod, knew nothing about this NEW king.

The king acted happy and said he would love to give a gift to this king. When these wise men found out where he was being born, they were to report back to King Harrod and let him know, so he too could give this king a special gift.

They left on good terms with the king and soon after leaving the palace, found the star again that they had lost in the first place which led them to King Harrod to ask for directions.

But, in their dreams, the star turned into an angel. And gave a warning to the wise men.

"Do not return to King Harrod! Go east for your return home. The gift Harrod has for the child is death."

At the same time the wise men were having their dream of a warning; Joseph too, was having a dream.

The darkness in his mind slowly turned to red fog. Then slowly a white figure appeared in angel form. The angel spoke, *"Do not stay here in Bethlehem. Take your family and flee to Egypt."*

By the time Joseph woke up, he was sweating from the dream. He looked out the window and saw all the caravan had gone. They left the land like nobody had ever been there.

That day Joseph was fixing up a wagon to carry all their furniture over bumpy roads. Mary obeyed her husband.

Meanwhile, at the Palace of King Harrod, the king called for his staff to be present.

"Counselors, I have a problem. Those wise men that were here two years ago left with valuable information they were to report back to me about where this . . . king was born. How long has it been?"

One of the members referred to a plant by the wall saying when they were here, that plant was small when they were here. It's one of those plants that grows an inch a year. Now it is two inches tall.

The king looked at the plant and it was indeed two inches tall.

"SO, THOSE WISE MEN ARE INDEED WISE.

HUMPH! I'LL SHOW THEM WHO'S WISE. THEY NEVER CAME BACK TO TELL ME OF THE LOCATION OF THE KING." King Harrod screamed. "Well, just in case, I wouldn't want to miss that child and deprive him of his . . . gift. So, I will give every boy child in that town the gift I was going to present the boy king."

He called all the soldiers to stand before his thrown.

"Now I'm a good king. Aren't I?"

The men shook their heads, yes. (More in fear than anything else, they didn't want to lose their heads.)

"Now let me see; what does one give a newborn king?

"I could give him gold, but I suppose those wise men have taken that gift to him already. I could give him shiny jewels. Babies love to play with sparkly things.

"No, that won't work if I gave him jewels, I would have to give ALL baby boys the same thing. . . and that could get expensive.

"What do you think?" he asked one of the soldiers.

He responded, "Clothes?"

"Then every boy child would be dressed in royal clothing. I don't want that to happen in Bethlehem. I don't want others to rival me, their king. After all, a king has a distinguished look.

By the way, have you kept your swords sharp?"

They all agreed they had, after all they were the king's army.

"That is good, men. Yes, really good." The king replied.

"Are your horses well fed?"

Once again, they nodded, they had.

"Good. Good. Now I want you to mount your horses and go into Bethlehem and give this newborn king my present."

His men began looking confused first at one another then at the king.

"Oh, I forgot to mention, what my gift is.

First of all, I will not have any other king in this town except for me.

So, I send out this command to ALL OF YOU. Kill every child under the age of two. Give them the gift of your sword upon their throats.

By doing this it will reassure me; that I am still king.

Now go."

Meanwhile, at the little white house Joseph had made a wagon to carry their items along with Mary and little boy Jesus.

"Bundle up, Mary, it's starting to get cold since the sun has gone down."

"Oh, Joseph, are you sure we are doing the right thing? I'm going to miss this place."

Chuckling, he replied, "You're not the only one who gets visited by a spirit. I told you the spirit came to me in a dream. It told me to move to Egypt. "

"Why?"

"I don't know. Perhaps something horrible is going to happen. Let's just do what the spirit has told me, and not ask questions."

"You're my husband, I shall obey."

With that Mary, Joseph, and Jesus under the cover of darkness travelled down the road to Egypt.

Little did the Christ family know what was about to take place.

As the family was exiting by way of the south road a hundred army men were entering Bethlehem by way of the north road. The people stood still at first in surprise. One of the soldiers held out a paper and read it out loud.

"TO ALL THE PEOPLE IN THE TOWN OF BETHLEHEM KING HARROD HAS A GIFT TO ALL THE BABY BOYS TWO YEARS AND UNDER."

With that, the men on horses withdrew their swords.

A little child looking up at them came to the heavy steel of the sword. The mother screamed and the father too tried to attack the soldier on horseback, but he too was hit in the head with the handle of the sword, falling to the earth like a thrown-away bag. The horses began to go through the town while women shouted and yelled in horrified grief. Many of the soldiers got off their horses and went for the cribs where a boy child lay. If they weren't sure if it were a boy they pulled its clothing off to reveal a boy. Many men fought with these soldiers but lost and were trampled underfoot. That was the worst day Bethlehem had ever seen. Night fell and there was much grieving in the town. Some of the soldiers in their hearts grieved what they had to do under the order of the king.

3

The road to Egypt was bumpy and harsh and it took about two days to arrive in a busy city of Egypt.

At first, the family had a hard time finding a place they could afford to live in. But finally, settled on a small house that had an extra room attached. Joseph could use this for his carpenter shop. The money from the kings allowed him to pay the rent.

A day or two later Joseph began to set up a carpentry business with his little helpers;

five-year-old Jesus and his little brother. They played in the wood shavings and scraps of wood more than they helped but Joseph got a big kick out of it and let them play. Both of them were his pride and joy. As they got older, the responsibility became a tad stronger. Occasionally, young Jesus would go and fetch water for his father. Of course, it started out to be a full cup but by the time Joseph got it, it was only half full.

After several years in Egypt, the Christ family was growing. Not only were the children becoming heavier but so was the house. Joseph made the back room his carpenter shop. More things were needed for the family. Like clothing. They grew out of their baby outfits faster than you can swat a fly. But thanks to the wise men, they had money to buy anything the kids and Mary needed.

Their clothing was the finest in the marketplace, that they could find. Mary was beautiful in blue.

All was going fine for the Christ family when one day, Mary came rushing home from shopping and cried out to Joseph. "Have you heard the news? It's horrifying!"

"Alright what sort of gossip have you been listening to this time?" Joseph asked with a smile.

"It's about King Harrod!" Mary was crying hard by now.

"King Harrod? What about King Harrod?"

Mary had a hard time talking but slowly managed to get the words out. "He's -he's-he is a murderer. A killer."

"Who doesn't know that? He has to kill his enemies to protect his kingdom."

"BABIES TOO?!"

"What..."

"What baby is going to attack HARROD? THEY'RE NOT HIS ENEMY! Tell me that, Joseph."

"What are you saying, Mary?"

"I'm telling you that King Harrod went into Bethlehem and killed every baby boy two years and younger. That would have been Jesus' age, at the time. There must have been thousands. Blood was everywhere."

"Oh!"

"Those poor mothers."

"Yes."

"I had no idea a king could be so cruel. Those poor, poor mothers and fathers."

Mary sat down with Joseph and cried her eyes out holding tightly to her sons. Joseph held all three of them in his arms.

Joseph got to thinking, "So that's why I dreamt what I dreamt. The angels were protecting Jesus from this horrid king."

"Is this" Mary sniffed, "an example of what his life is going to be like for our boy?" She cried on Joseph's shoulders.

"I'm afraid so. Don't look at it from the bad side. Look at it from the good side. God doesn't trust everyone to babysit his son. He trusted us. Would his father in heaven allow harm to come to his son Jesus?"

Bethlehem was never the same the wailing could be heard for a long time after. Time passed and the king's horrible deed was recorded for all history to be learned about.

Jesus and his brothers were getting to an age where they could help around the house more, by doing odd chores and helping their father in the carpentry shop. By now water given to Joseph was a full cup instead of a half one.

Jesus, the older brother, now got to the stage in his life where he learned to play tricks on his brothers. One time he called his brothers into the room, then challenged them with a little bet. "Hold out your hands, palm side down," he told them.

They did. Then Jesus produced four cups of water.

"See these cups? Well, I'm going to place them on top of the back of your hand. Your part is to balance them and not spill them. If you spill them, you will be known as a frog for the rest of the day. Got it?"

They all agreed. Laughing.

The two brothers put their hands out and then Jesus gently put the cups on the back of their hands. "You're pretty good at this," he commented. "You sure you've never done this before?"

The brothers shook their heads, no.

Once the cups were secured and on top of the back of their hands, the brothers were doing their best not to spill a drop, Jesus got up and leaving the room replied, "I don't know about you guys, but it's a nice day, I'm going out to play."

Not wanting to be known as frogs the two brothers sat there looking at one another, dumbfounded.

Joseph's business began to grow as well as his family. Mary now had a girl.

People where wanting doors put on their houses, a table with chairs built, and even out houses to be built way out back. Joseph kept his money in wooden boxes in the back of their house. It was in these same boxes that he kept the gold given to Jesus when he was a baby.

The gold came in handy for when the time for taxes came about each year; he had it. It also was useful when it came to buying clothes, and even buying a nice wagon pulled by two mules to get around town. He only got those coins of gold when needed.

While the children were growing up, they learned the carpenter business. It started with them retrieving cups of water from the bucket. As they got older, they had to fetch water out of the Rosetta River. This was dangerous, there were alligators in that water. But once a month they heard of some women going down to the river to wash their clothes and get eaten by one of these beasts. Of course, they had to watch out for alligators because those horrible critters built nests on the bank of that river.

The more the children grew up, the more responsibility was given to them by their father. Sometimes they had to carry chairs or a table out to a wagon to get it ready to be delivered as the boys were older now and could carry a table or chairs.

Joseph and Mary noticed how fast their children were growing. By now she was expecting another child. Every day Mary sent the little girl into the field to pick wildflowers to place them in the window or on the table.

One day a rider came galloping through the town, dust was everywhere. He had a message, for the town's folk.

KING HARROD WAS DEAD.

4

For some reason, all of Bethlehem had false crocodile tears over the death of King Harrod. Even though they acted like they were filled with remorse; the truth was they were happy his days of ruling finally came to an end. For years they lived in fear of that king's rulership but now he was dead. They all felt the freedom of joy.

Don't take me wrong, they were still angry at the mass murder of innocent babies.

While they had yet to get a new ruler for the town, the government continued as it always had. With the ugly spirit lifted off their backs, the people worked with a happy attitude. In fact, people while passing by would say a friendly hello to each other.

Another year went by and Jesus reached the age of exploring. He liked to travel but his folks thought of him to be too young without a buddy to go with him. He began by exploring the tree in his yard. Making a house made from his father's used lumber in the backyard.

Of course, he helped his father as much as he could by delivering furniture. But in idle times he worked on the tree house. His brothers and sisters helped.

There were times when his duty was done at the shop and he didn't feel like working on the tree house, so he went out into the crowded streets of Egypt. There were times mischief befell this almost teen.

While in the marketplace, he loved hiding amongst the robes hanging on lines that the vendors put up to be able to sell their wares. He'd slip in and out of them. He'd hide for a while then pop out to see if anyone was looking, hoping to scare them. Many times, he failed and the customer would slap Jesus. Even when the owners saw him, they pretended not to see him. They knew this kid was harmless. Then he'd go back into hiding. For some reason he loved the cloth brushing over his face.

As he was going in and out of the wardrobe, he suddenly felt something on his foot that stopped him in his tracks. He whipped the robe back to find it was a girl standing on one of his feet.

Surprised he asked, "Who are you?"

"I'm called Sarah. What's your name?"

"Jesus. And that's my foot you're on."

"Oops. Sorry," she said.

Jesus looked at the girl. She had big brown eyes, black hair and olive-coloured skin. He was breathless.

"You want to come home with me and we'll play. I got two brothers there as well."

"Okay, Sarah," he said.

On the way back to her house they encountered two beggars on the street. Both of them holding a bowl in the children's faces. One asked, "Can you please spare a copper? I have not eaten in days."

The other beggar dressed about the same, very poorly just held a cup up to them. And said nothing.

Both children had nothing but a few pieces of candy in their purses. Jesus dropped it into the beggar's cup who spoke.

The other one he gave nothing because he had nothing more, to give.

They were dirty looking and their skin and hair had dried mud settled in their pores. Even their whiskers were unkept. The man who got none gave Jesus a dirty look.

So, Sarah and Jesus went to Sarah's house to play. They played on a wagon in her backyard. Jesus gave them a push while her brothers sat in it laughing. They were all having fun. Soon Jesus was tired and pushed the wagon into the shade of a tree and sat down on a rock.

The four of them began to talk. First of nothing at all, then one of the brothers mentioned he had seen strange lights in the sky day before yesterday. He said they all flew over Egypt. "I got scared."

"Scared of what?" Jesus asked.

"The lights in the skies."

"Why do you fear them?"

"Because there were strange lights up there. What could they be?"

"Perhaps they were angles frying by. They do have other places to be than just Earth."

The brother seemed to relax, then.

"Sarah I'm going to speak in the temple tomorrow. I'll be twelve years old; you want to come and listen to me?" In his heart, he was hoping for her to say yes.

She agreed. And Jesus was very happy.

It was getting late in the day and Jesus had to return home. On his way, he met the beggar he had given the candy to.

He greeted Jesus with a happy smile. "That

candy, you gave me earlier. Where did you get it? What did you put in it?"

Jesus just listened to the man.

"You gave me that candy early in the day and I have given some to everyone I met. See here." He held up his cup and Jesus saw it was full. Jesus took one.

The man once again asked, "How did you do that?"

Jesus just smiled and continued to walk in the direction of his home.

The beggar looked on astonished at the weird kid called Jesus.

Meeting him at the steps of the temple Sarah waited. Finally, she saw a young man heading her way. Dressed in a silky robe with curls brushed out and made to look good for the rabbi.

"What are you going to speak on?"

"I don't have the foggiest idea. But we shall see."

"You mean you have prepared nothing?"

"Nope. My heart will do all the talking." He smiled.

The temple, from the outside, was huge and beautiful. There were four giant figureheads sitting there staring at the people. A door was opened at the base of the temple. People were walking into the great temple. The roof had a gold dome on top of it. Its white walls were made of marble with green vines growing all over.

The insides were even more breathtaking than the outside.

Twelve giant columns lined the hall and each one had paintings on them. Beautiful candles lined the walls. Rabbis walked around in there breathtaking adornments looking as pious as can be.

Jesus before he entered notice a Rabbi turning a beggar away. It must have been the way he was dressed and the Rabbi figured the guy had no money.

"What's different between the beggars outside and the rabbis in there?" Jesus thought.

As he went inside there were all sorts of gadgets. He knew this from the other times he had gone to the temple, but this time he noticed them all the more. A bowl for holy water, candles to be lit for the poor souls, and a box in the corner to tell the Rabbi what you did last week.

A Rabbi approached him and asked, "Is your name Jesus?"

Politely, Jesus answered, "Yes."

The gruff Rabbi shifted a sneer at the boy. "According to your mother and father, you are twelve? Is that correct?"

"Yes."

"Where are they?"

"My father couldn't make it because he has some deliveries today. And my mother couldn't make it due to all my brothers and sisters."

The Rabbi said no more but asked one more question. "So, what are you going to speak on when it's time for you to give your speech?"

Jesus thought about it for a bit then answered: "How money, is so needed."

"A good topic. Okay, wait over there with those other parishioners."

He took a seat on a bench next to an older man.

The man smiled at Jesus and introduced his self as, John.

Jesus did the same.

The man coughed and then spoke again, "Dang this cough. I wish it would just go away."

"It can; if you have faith enough."

"I have been coming to this temple for twenty years and that's all they preach about is you donate your money God will give you a blessing. Well, that is what I have done. I have given so much money to this church I'm almost bankrupt and I still have that cough."

"But God doesn't ask for money. He gives his blessings free of charge. All you have to do is have faith in him."

"Then why does the Rabbi tell a different story?"

"Have you looked at their lifestyle?"

"Come to think of it . . . no I haven't."

At this time Jesus was called to the alter to give his speech.

Jesus just smiled as he left the man, pondering.

He stood there and faced the audience without any fear. Looking around the room he saw everyone staring at him and behind him sat five Rabbis, they too were staring at him.

Jesus looked out into the audience and began his speech; "First of all, I would like to thank you for coming out to day. It is a beautiful day to praise the Lord. But I have a question. Did you come here to give honour to God or did you come because of a tradition of doing it every Sunday?

Ya 'know these Rabi' look into the rolls of scriptures and deliver to you what they think God wants you to hear. But many who come just sit there and don't do a thing about it. When they exit, ask them what was told to them from the altar they give you a blank stare and say, "I don't know."

The audience was giving ear to what Jesus was speaking.

"Why come at all and waste a few hours? Take notes; love thy neighbour. How many really go over to their neighbours just to have a chit-chat with them?"

The Rabbis looked at the boy giving him approval. So, the lad went on.

"Yesterday I and a friend were walking down the street when a beggar approached us, asking for money. Now, we didn't have to give him anything, but if we hadn't, we would have felt bad. Soon after several Rabbis walked by us and they were dressed in the finest wardrobe. Comparing it with the beggars' clothes.

Then I got to thinking about how can the temple have so much money and a dome of gold that sits on the roof. Where did that come from? I'll tell you. Your purses. Granted the church needs your money to keep the candles burning and pay for the lot fees and they have mortgages, just to give you a place to come and remind you to worship.

But the church has so much that many of you give way more than you should. Instead, why don't you give your money to these beggars or give them bread instead of coins?

Your neighbours, need it more than those who preach here. Oh sure, you can argue the fact, If I give them money, they don't spend it on food. Heed not what they do with your money that's up to them. It matters that God saw your heart and your intention."

By now the Rabbis became more interested in his speech.

"Basically, what I'm saying to you is why give your money to the church when there are so many in your neighbourhood that can use your money more than the temple."

Suddenly a bang was heard, startling Jesus.

"How dare you!" A Rabbi yelled.

"You are inciting the people against the temple."

Jesus turned in time to see all the Rabbis getting out of their seats and coming towards him.

Before he could defend himself, he was lifted off the altar and in a manner of a few moments Jesus was thrown out of the Temple down those wide staircases. Falling head over heal he landed on his stomach in a puddle of mud. The nice clothes he had bought just for the occasion were ruined. While people were laughing Sarah came rushing up to his side and helped him up.

"Well, I think I know what they thought of my speech.

Looking at his scraped-up legs and bruised arms Sarah commented; "Are you sure you're alright?"

"Don't worry. I got a lot of myrrh at home, given to me as a baby."

The two of them talked and laughed as Jesus limped home.

5

∞

Sarah walked Jesus home, feeling sorry for that incident at the temple. She had much talk, with him, about how mean it was to throw him out of the temple. That's not the only event that happened that day in Bethlehem. The place, the former home of the Christ family was about to get a new king, King Archelaus.

This king was not like his predecessor, who had been cruel, greedy, and jealous. This new king was handsome and had a head for governing the people. He also had a trait the other king didn't. He had a kind heart.

But unfortunately, his son Prince Rau was the opposite of his father. He was not only a brat but also, very spoiled. Many times, he would demand things and would bully his staff who was already waiting on him. So spoiled was he, that he was considered by the staff to be lazy as well, and wouldn't dress without one of his fathers' servants, dressing him. He wouldn't even consider removing a robe without the hands of servants. At times his table manners were just as rude. It wasn't that he was a bad person, I would say it was because his father spoiled him. I believe the reason was that the king had but one son and so gave into Prince Rau's demands.

Even though he had classes in swordsmanship, he would often sneak out of the castle and go among the common folks. He did this by digging a hole with his sword out back of the palace. Three large trees hid him from view, as he managed to dig a hole large enough for his torso to slip through. Once outside the stone fence, he'd ride to town and sometimes cause

Havoc, then he would return to the castle before anyone would notice.

At times Jesus would play with his brothers and other times he would lose himself in working around his father's shop.

Jesus was well-liked by his family and everyone who came in contact with him. They found him to be kind, friendly, and always willing to help someone out. He made an easy adjustment to living in Egypt. Being there he found so many opportunities to learn the cultures of many nations and also speak in foreign tongues.

Every year a new brother or sometimes a sister would grace the Christ household. But Jesus didn't mind, he loved his brothers and sisters.

But one time, a tragedy happened. Mary had a baby that was lifeless. Both Mary and

Joseph and the family were sad at the still-born child and weeping.

Jesus looked over in the direction of the breathless child laying on a blanket. While his mother was crying and his father holding onto her for comfort.

Jesus reached over and touched the head of his breathless brother, with a lot of compassion in his heart. No one noticed, but a miracle was about to happen. Breath entered the baby and his heart began to thump. A few moments later, a loud cry was coming out of the baby.

Surprised, Mary rushed into the room and grabbed hold of her now-breathing, new born baby. She ran and picked him up then hugged him ever so tightly. Tears formed in her eyes while Joseph comforted her over the baby, now alive.

Jesus looked up at them and smiled as his parents held his baby brother in their arms, not even realizing Jesus had saved his life. Then he went back to playing.

That night Joseph lay near his wife and fell into a deep sleep. He began to move his head right and left and soon his whole body was tossing and turning. In his dream, he saw a beautiful light and slowly an angel appeared.

"JOESPH YOU AND YOUR FAMILY WILL FIND IT SAFE NOW. KING HARROD IS NOW DEAD. YOU MAY RETURN WITH SAFTY. BY YOU RETURNING TO NAZARUS THEY WILL SOON CALL YOUR SON A NAZARINE."

The angel faded into memory.

The next morning, Joseph told Mary about his dream and she being a good wife said, "If the angel told you to go there, then we must do so. You are my husband, I will obey."

With that, he gave her a kiss on the forehead.

That afternoon Jesus and his friend, Sarah went down to the Nile for a swim. It was cool and refreshing out of the hot sun and in fact, the sun had warmed up the water so swimming was pleasant. They just had to be careful of alligators.

Sarah looked up to Jesus because he was deeply a smart person and at times did things that she couldn't explain. She was falling in love with him at the same time trying to figure him out.

They pulled themselves up near the shore ad got out of the cart.

"I can't be here too long," Sarah spoke first, "I have to do my chores. But my mother said I could go for a short time. She never would have let me go if she knew I was swimming with you, Jesus."

"How come?"

"Because you're a boy, silly."

"He that breaks traditions advances the world."

"Huh?"

"I'm just saying, too many people follow tradition to a fault. They miss the real focus that God wants them to see.

People do what someone before them has done for a long time. In other words; tradition. They aren't watching things they should be watching but instead are watching the way their ancestors have done it for years. God wants you to focus on him; not on tradition laid down by your forefathers. As long as you're not committing bad ways, its's fun to learn new things by breaking traditions.

Well, Sarah, I had a lot of fun swimming with you but now I got to go help my father in the carpenter shop."

Sarah watched as Jesus faded off in the distance heading towards his home knowing little that would be the last time she saw him.

When he got home his parents told him the news about their moving. In a way, he was sad because he would have to leave his friends behind. Moving for a child is usually hard on them, it means that their world is about to change.

Mary cleaned out the house and you could hear echoing as they spoke coming from the empty room. They said goodbye to their friends and neighbours and began the long trip back to Nazarus where Mary's family lived.

6

The road to Nazarus was long, tiring, and hot. It took a few days to reach its enormous boarders. There were big hills dotted with trees and so many people lived in stone houses one next to each other.

An aroma of freshly baked bread entered their nostrils. Mary's mother a baker did wonders with the dough.

"We're almost there, Joseph. We are almost there." Mary said excitedly. Finally, they reached the home where Mary grew up and her mother was still living there. Behind the counter of the bakery, her mother looked up and was surprised to see her daughter. Both of them gave each other a hug. There's something about a grandma's hug you never forget but treasure it always. Her grandchildren took an instant liking to her. Even Joseph got in on the action and gave her a hug. She ran a bakery shop and for a dozen grandchildren that was just fine.

Jesus seemed to be the one that stood out from the rest of the family. He was always doing things to help out even before he was asked to do something. He set up the table for food and when the meal was over would get up and clean off the table and do dirty dishes.

One day the grandmother asked him why he did it because she had lived a long life and had never seen any ten-year-old doing that. Not that it's a bad thing, mind you.

His reply was a good one; "I find it best to serve people. You get them in a better mood when you wait on them. Not as a slave but as someone who cares about them."

Then Jesus took two big cookies off the shelf and walked off leaving his grandmother stunned.

Again, she was left talking to herself saying she never met anyone like him before.

Joseph made room in the back of the shop for his carpentry work, right next to the grandma's oven where she made her baked goods.

Many times, Jesus in the morning, would help his father, put legs on stools and chairs. But

The heat became unbearable from not only the oven but also from the sun. Joseph gave Jesus the time in the afternoon to do as he pleased. That's when he and his brothers and sisters would go for a swim at a nearby water hole.

A wooden plank was pushed out over the water it was weighed down by some heavy rocks. It was fun to jump off it into the water. All afternoon they played alligator attack; a fun game to play. To play it you had to be in the water watching out for a person who played the part of the alligator who would slip under water then from below grabbed an ankle. Then you'd have to try and get free from his grasp. Sometimes They'd splash water at each other and the best fun was king of the mound, where you stood on a mound of dirt until someone came up behind you and pushed you into the water. Then you tried to regain your position back on the mound by pushing him into the water. Whoever was on the mound when they'd get tired of that game was 'KING OF THE MOUND.'

It was at one of these swimming sessions Jesus met a new friend. His name was Lazarus.

Lazarus was like Jesus in many ways. He was a listener; he was gentle and very kind.

And the best part he didn't live too far from Jesus.

There were times Jesus and Lazarus would play ball with a pig's bladder for hours until it was time to return to the shop.

In time, Jesus and Lazarus became really good friends. Sometimes Lazarus would come to the shop and help out his friend. He enjoyed painting so Joseph allowed him to paint the table and chairs the color of red.

Lazarus said, "I'd be happy to do it, Mr. Christ."

"I got to run to the market for a bit and I'll be back as soon as I can."

Both Jesus and Lazarus said, "Okay."

For the next few hours the boys worked steadily at the shop and did a lot of small talking.

Then Lazarus asked a strange question, "Ever had a girlfriend, Jesus?"

"Sure, I have."

"What is her name?"

"Sarah. But I had to leave her behind when we moved out of Egypt."

"Was she nice?"

"I thought so." Turing the conversation back towards Lazarus, asked, "How about you?"

"OH, yeah. I got one. But she's always busy on the farm."

"The reason I don't see her too much lately is because I lied to her."

"That, you should never have done. Lying is a bad thing."

"Why?"

"When you lie to one, you kill the trust of many. When you kill the trust of many, they never look at you with the same respect again."

"You're so right. How do I make amends."

"Go say you're sorry you lied. It's a step in the right direction."

"I'll do that."

It was at this moment a rather large puppy rushed into the room. He leapt all over the room excitedly. Wagging his tail. He jumped on the table Lazarus was working on and spilt the paint, red paint all over. He jumped up on Jesus, as he came through the door. They tried to capture him but he slipped out of their hands. He licked and licked the faces of the boys as they tried their best to catch him. All the commotion before him sent him in a state of shock. A dog running free, boys chasing a dog, red paw paints everywhere. Who would ever believe this was actually taking place right here in grandmas' bakery? So, he began to laugh. They were all laughing.

Joseph tried to catch the dog too but it slipped through his hands. Not only did it knock him off balance but turned him into red from the paint that rubbed off his fur. The dog ran through the door that led to the bakery. Suddenly nothing was safe. The grandmother yelled out and so did Mary. Like her husband, she too tried to catch the dog but ended up getting red paint not only on her but also on the baked goods. Grandma as well joined everyone in trying to trap the dog in a corner but he was a jumper as well as fast. Grandma was trying to grab the loaves of bread before this playful dog landed on them as well. Too late. The dog knocked the bread to the ground. Customers entered the bakery and turn tail and went through the door they had just come in. The brown dog now red with paint also ran through the same door and down the street following the customer.

Joseph looked at the mess. Red paint was everywhere including the bread most of it on the floor dripping with red paint.

Grandmother knowing how young children love dogs immediately blamed this incident on the boys.

"Where is my switch? I'll show those boys how not to let a dog into this shop! Look! Just look at all my bakery goods. A whole day's work gone in a blink of an eye."

Joseph had to step in to protect his boys. "It wasn't them. If anyone deserves a switch to his backside, it would be me. I brought the dog home for the boys, but now I see I was all wrong. Never knew he had so much energy. Go take a walk and cool off. I'll clean up, here."

She did just that, she took a walk and didn't speak a word to the man.

Joseph picked up dishes, pots, pans and anything else that had red paint on it. Jesus and his friend Lazarus were already cleaning the carpenter's shop. It took most of the night to clean it. The shop and bakery remained closed the next day. But eventually, Grandmother and Mary started to bake again. The carpenter's shop too, was back in order.

The funny thing, they never did find that dog. I have a hunch they never tried.

7

No one seems to notice time rolling on except for those who have already passed most of their life and wonder where did it go? The children were getting bigger and stronger now. Jesus was 16 by now and with his friend, Lazarus had fun in the afternoon. Of course, the morning hours were dedicated to the shop while the afternoon was their time.

Joseph had bought a bigger house because they moved out of the bakery. The reason why this happened was because the grandmother had been getting complaints that her bread was tasting like sawdust. She knew where to lay the blame.

Joseph had sawdust and tools next to her oven. So, she simply asked them to move. Which they did and they bought a house in the country next to a wheat field.

The afternoons were the children's time to go and play. They made up games and played old ones like tag, you're it, or went exploring in the area of the woods that was a small distance from their house.

One thing Lazarus noticed about Jesus was that he was a loner. His brothers and sisters didn't agree with his ideas of philosophy. And at times, he'd do things that gave his friend a double take and that his friend couldn't explain so they began calling him the odd ball. Not that Jesus was mean to his brothers and sisters. In fact, quite the contrary.

On their way into the field, they picked up rocks and threw them as far as they could.

Before long it became a competition of who could throw the farthest, then who was best at hitting targets. Eventually, the rocks turned into clots of dirt. Then each person was the target. As the dirt hit the intended person, it would break off into dust clouds. Even Jesus hit his brother with a dirt clog and in retaliation threw two of the biggest ones he could find at Jesus.

All of them were laughing. Jesus spoke up and said you never know who you're throwing at.

A few of his brothers said, "Huh?"

"You know, 'dust thou art to dust returneth.'"

Once again, he received a, "Huh?"

"If you would look in your scriptures once in a while, you would see that's what it says."

Then one of his brothers commented, "Those are nothing but words written down."

"But did you ever think, those words were written for a reason?"

"Yeah, but they can't be proven."

"Oh really?"

"Yeah, really!"

"Okay. I'll prove it to you." Jesus said standing off a rock. "Take your arms and hold it in front of your face."

They all did it.

"Now with your other hand, rub it back and forth on that arm."

Intrigued, they did as they were told. Before long tiny flakes of skin which appeared as dust floated to the ground.

"He's right." A sister proclaimed.

Next thing the children were rubbing their heads with the same reaction. They were making a game of it.

"So, those dust clogs are people who have lived here a long time ago. So you see, you never know who you are throwing at."

Jesus continued to walk in the farmer's field. Along a path between the woods and the field itself, Lazarus followed and then eventually the children followed.

They went a quarter of a mile and Lazarus noticed another path made by smaller animals like rabbits or chipmunks. Let's follow."

"Okay."

The woods were getting a shade darker now.

Soon all were enjoying this adventure. They didn't mind going through these tall trees that provided lots of cool shades and branches to climb on. They leapt over hallowed logs but came to a stop when they saw a huge tree in the clearing.

This tree was just what the children ordered. It was tall and had low branches. The other trees surrounding it were made like a fort. There were plenty of wildflowers of different colours for the girls to pick. Also, with the boys, you know how noisy boys can be. When they climbed the tree to its highest branch and yelled, their voices would bounce off nearby trees.   It was a rather large tree from side to side. It had two branches that hung low where they could get their start for climbing it. Its bark was thick and grooved up and down the dark trunk. Green leaves sprouted out of every branch.

The children wasted no time climbing it. The older boys raced to the top while the girls rather gossiped on lower branches or gathered wildflowers.

The view from the tree was spectacular.

They could see a nearby swamp on one side, and on the other side was the field from which they had just come.

Later, like the girls, the boys got tired of climbing and sat down on their branch. The boys talked about who was best in the gladiator ring and who was best at cart races. While the girls talked about baking bread and things they needed to do around the house. Eventually, the boys slithered down the trunk of the tree and joined the girls in their conversation. Soon the conversation led to talking about the tree they had discovered.

"What should we do with this tree?"

"I know," shouted one of the girls. "Let's turn it into a tree house."

"That's a great idea." Shouted one of the boys.

"But we have our duties at home."

"Let's skip out of them."

"A man, who skips out on work will soon find his plate will have less food," Jesus remarked.

"We'll come in the afternoon when our work is done and when we have pleased our parents."

Soon the children were bringing knives and hammers from home. They began by cutting off small branches from the big ones. By doing that, they got a better view of the surrounding area, trees, the swamp, and the field. Jesus and Lazarus brought wood left behind at the carpenter's shop.

"They'll provide a platform high in the tree by laying them across two branches."

The low branches will supply steps to get to the above branches.

The rest of the day, the children had so much fun with this tree. In time, the hot afternoon became cool again, and the children knew it was time to get back home. All were having fun and before they knew it the time had gone by rapidly. Looking up the tree trunk to the crown of branches overhead, they watched in awe the squirrels above leaping from branch to branch, you could tell they were having fun. But now it was time to go home and do the evening chores.

Lazarus, from a branch at the bottom of the tree, saw Jesus at the top. Figuring it would take a few moments for Jesus to get down from up there, called out to him. Lazarus looked up again to see if he could see his friend but he was nowhere to be seen. He heard a voice right next to him.

It was Jesus. "Let's go."

Stunned to see his friend next to him, when two seconds ago he was at the top of the tree, when he knew it would take at least a few minutes to reach his buddy. He was suddenly next to Lazarus. In shock, he asked, "How did you do that?"

"Do what?"

"I saw you high up there and now you are next to me. You couldn't have crawled down that tree that fast."

Jesus smiled and headed for home.

"You sure are weird," Lazarus mumbled.

8

∞

Mary Looking out the window wondered if her husband wasn't spending Jesus' investment rather fast; bought a big house after they got kicked out from her mother because of the dog incident.

The house they lived in, now, is huge and expensive. Not to mention the clothing her children wore, the best in town.   S h e pondered all this in her heart. She didn't dare mention it to her husband because it was not her place to question her husband.

It was morning and Mary was making breakfast, while Joseph was making a doorway, the children were still sleeping on the floor, and Jesus was sweeping out the shop; Lazarus came barging in with something in his hand.

Mary remarked, "I see it must be time for breakfast. Morning Lazarus."

"Morning Mrs. Christ. Where's Jesus?"

"Out back in the shop."

He quickly ran through the curtained door to the shop and caught Jesus and Joseph by surprise.

"Look what's coming to town!" He turned and saw Joseph then remembered his manners, "Oh, morning, Mr. Christ."

"Morning, Lazarus. So, I see it's time for breakfast," he said smiling, "What is the excitement?"

"A festival, Mr. Christ. Right here in Nazarus."

Jesus got excited as well. "How far away is it?"

"Not far. Three miles at the most."

"I got to finish my work here . . ."

"I'll help you."

Joseph, looking at the two boys, cleared his throat as if to say, 'Aren't you forgetting something?'

Jesus knew what it was. He didn't ask for permission from his father, "Father, can I go to the festival?"

Taking his fingers around his chin, Lazarus with his brown eyes looked at Joseph, and asked, "Please."

"Okay. Okay. You worked hard enough, Jesus. You can go."

"Oh, thank you, Father." Lazarus caught himself. "I mean, Mr. Christ."

On the way to the festival, they came upon a stream of water that hippos used at times, today, not a huge hippo could be seen. To cross the stream without getting wet they would have to walk around this steam of water a few miles out of the way. Lazarus looked upon it and said, "Well, time for a swim."

Jesus chuckled, "No need." He continued over the water and Lazarus looked on in amazement. Jesus walked on top of the water while his friend swam across.

"How are you doing that!" surprised, Lazarus shouted.

"Doing what, Lazarus?"

"Walking on water!"

"Oh, that." Jesus never answered the question. He turned to his friend and smiled. He then continued to the bank on the opposite side of the stream and when Lazarus got out of the water he walked toward the festival.

The boys were excited that they were going to the festival. Many folks were already there with all sorts of folks. There were fat ones, thin ones, good-looking ones, ugly ones. Plenty of attractions to see, rides to ride, not to mention food stands, and animal displays.

"Where shall we go, first?" Lazarus asked excitedly looking at the festival.

"Let's go check out the rides."

As they were rounding one of the corners Jesus bumped into a man. Jesus quickly apologized. The man said nothing but held him by the shoulders.

"Let me go, I said I was sorry."

"No. No. Wait a second. Don't I know you?"

Jesus and the man looked at each other.

"Oh-h-h-h, I know you," the man said. "You're the boy at the temple. I'm the one who had the cough. Remember?"

Jesus looked for a moment then it dawned on him. "Oh, you're the man I saw at the temple."

"That's right. And you were right."

"Yes, I know."

"The cough is gone. I haven't coughed since that day. And another thing."

Jesus asked, "What?"

"I watched them throw you out of the temple that day. When they threw you out, I decided that's not a place for me, so, I haven't been back since."

"Sir, you are as wise as a serpent and as smart as an owl." Jesus spoke, "Every day is another day for learning and the best tool I know of is making mistakes. Have a good day."

"You sure are smart for a young man." With those words, the men turned toward the food place at the festival and waved a friendly goodbye.

Jesus waved back.

Lazarus getting Jesus' attention pointed to the rides and one particular one, a wooden horse which hung from a tree branch. It was secured by ropes to each end of the horse. One was tied to the head while the other was tied to the tail.

Once a person sat on the wooden horse, both men pulled the ropes hard while the horse bucked. The person on it struggled to stay on. Bouncing and weaving vigorously jerking until the person fell off.

Lazarus said let's go on that one. Referring to the wood horse.

"Ok," Jesus said.

Lazarus was next to get on this challenging ride. With the aid of one of the workers, he managed to get in the seat. At first, he waved at Jesus with a smile, then grabbed the ropes laying on the horse in front of him. Suddenly without warning the two men began yanking and tugging the wooden horse hard.

Lazarus was jolted forward and backwards then side to side; then back again. It was too much for him and the ropes slipped out of his hands and he thumped loudly on the ground knocking the breath out of him.

Jesus was laughing so hard that he barely made it to the wooden horse. One of the men hauled Lazarus to the sideline, away from the horse so others could get on. The other man prepared Jesus on the wooden animal and placed the ropes in his hands.

"Your friend is okay," said the man who aided Lazarus. Jesus then took the end of his rope and waved to the man with the other rope. Signalling he was ready. They began to pull hard on their ropes and the horse began to jerk.

Meanwhile, unbeknownst to Jesus and Lazarus, three figures in the crowd stood watching the boys' making fools of themselves.

Two of these mysterious folks wore cheap loin clothes and draped in cheaper robes. While the one in the middle of these three had rich clothing on. They watched as Jesus bobbed to and fro and then finally fell off, with a crash to the ground. Not wanting anyone to know of his hurt, put on a fake laughing spree. Lazarus laughed with him.

But these three strangers looked on with interest.

Both teens were rubbing their rumps as they walked with a limp away from this wooden horse ride. Next they decided to go see what else this festival had to offer.

Next, they headed for the food stands where a pie-eating contest was about to commence. Looking at each other they both found a stool and sat at the table provided for the contest. Looking down the line, they saw that man he met at the temple.

The two waved at each other.

Other contestants were ready to bite into the pie in front of them. There was an assortment of apple, cherry, and blueberries.

The contestants watched as the hostess gave the instructions. "Before you, is one fruit pie. You must devour your pie without using your hands. . ."

"What about our feet," someone interrupted.

After the laughter died down the hostess replied, "No."

"The first one finished wins a gold coin."

Not far away those three teens were watching the guys.

It will start with the word "go." The hostess began to count. "One, two, three, go!"

The contestants slammed their heads into the pie before them. Each, taking big bites that their mouth would allow chewed it rapidly and swallowed and went back for another bite doing this as fast as they could going back for another bite. Their faces were becoming blue, and red depending on the fruit in the pie.

Pieces of pie flew every which way as the contestants continued to go back for more until their pie was consumed.

Soon one of the contestants stood up indicating his pie was finished.

"The winner!" the hostess said. Walked over and gave the man his coin.

Jesus and Lazarus looked at each other and laughed so hard that they fell off their stools. Both of them including all the contestants' faces were a mess. But no one cared.

Standing near, the three mysterious guys were still observing both Lazarus and Jesus. As soon as everyone was done, they all left to go to other parts of the festival.

They passed by a booth where a Rabbi announcing his heart out telling his god was the only one.

A few booths down from his booth was a priest saying that his God was the true way to heaven.

And still, another booth across from his lay scripture thumper relating God was theirs.

Jesus just shook his head and kept on walking.

Lazarus came up beside Jesus and asked a simple question, "If their God is the only and that one has the only god not to mention that person way down there also claims to have the only true god. How do you know which to choose from?"

"A very good question. If you read the scriptures, it tells you that there is one God, not five or twenty."

Just then the two heard the baying of sheep.

9

The sound of sheep came from around the corner. The two went to check it out. There were sheep penned in a coral. Little did they know they were being followed.

They watched as Jesus and Lazarus climbed on the fence to touch the soft woolly animals.

A man opening the gate to let them out said, "You can follow us to the field. It's time for their demonstration." The man blew on a horn three times, letting everyone know the demonstration was about to commence. So, the two boys followed the man and his sheep.

While waiting Jesus looked out over the white woolly animal, and went into a daydream.

The dream reminded him of a place where there was no evil.

"Hey, remember me, your friend?" Lazarus. "What are you dreaming about?"

"Sorry, the white fleece on their back got me thinking. Sorry. But I was just thinking of a place called Heaven. A place where there is no such thing as sickness and a place where there were no more wars. Everyone lives in this large place. And has Mansions and is served good food by spirits."

"Well, you know what I want. That is for you to tell me how you walked on that water back there."

Jesus just smiled at his friend and then returned to watching the sheep.

There were other spectators gathered now at the wooden fence. More and more came. It seemed like the whole festival was here.

The sheep ran around the small field directed by a barking dog. The shepherd was good at training animals.

They would run to the far end of the field and at the blow of a whistle, turn and come running to their master. They did this and many more tricks in all.

"Look at those sheep run," Lazarus pointed out to Jesus. "No wolf will eat those sheep."

Under the command of one person, the sheep went this way and that. They did circles around the shepherd who was in charge of them.

Suddenly from behind a rock a man jumped up trying to get the animal's attention, by waving a red cloth. But it was of no use, the leader of the shepherd gave a sharp whistle, twice, and the sheep turned and ran back to the stall from which they came.

The audience gave a big round of applause.

"I wonder how he did that?" Lazarus asked.

"It's simple, Lazarus," Jesus spoke. "Sheep know their master's voice and listen to it. The stranger's voice and action were different from the way they had been taught.

Therefore, that voice was a stranger to those animals and thus did not obey that man's command.

Let this be a lesson to you, Lazarus. If you ever become a leader of people who are following your leadership, like a Rabbi, take care of your flock. Watch over them. Let them get to know you. If not, the wolf will lead them away for his dinner."

"You're so smart. I'm glad you're my friend."

The two departed the sheep demonstration to go look at the other parts of the festival but strangely enough, no one was around. All the festival folks including the vendors were there watching the sheep demonstration.

The teens were now talking small talk and got around to ask about his father Joseph.

"He's just my stepfather, but I love him very much. You know, I feel as if I'm here on this planet to do great things yet I feel I'm in training. I also feel a day will come and man will destroy this earth and only a handful will be saved. It will be hell, with no way to escape. But a place called Heaven will touch this planet briefly, and so fast like a twinkle in an eye that a few will be saved from the fire."

As they were walking three young men were approaching Jesus and Lazarus at a rapid pace. Just then a shove came from behind Jesus. It was so hard it knocked him over. He hit his knees on the ground and he sprawled out. His hands caught his fall but because of the loose gravel, he spread out. Not knowing what just happened Jesus tried to get up but the bully stepped on his hands so he couldn't. Jesus couldn't get back up. Lazarus noticed this and gave the bully a hard shove back and he landed in the pottery booth, knocking a few of the wonderful pieces down as they hit the ground.

As Jesus got back up, two arms grabbed Lazarus around the waist and hauled him back into a tree pinning him there with his face facing forward.

The bully who was thrown into the pot booth now looked around at everyone with a mean face then he noticed Lazarus pinned to the tree. The bully's hand formed a fist, then started to run toward the captive, with full force. Not thinking he released his foot off of Jesus' hand and he leapt up at a remarkable speed.

Lazarus saw the bully coming towards him closed his eyes and braced his face for the blow.

Jesus bounced up grabbing the bully's elbow and managed to turn this bad boy around messing up his chance to land his fist in Lazarus' face. The other two bullies continued to hold Lazarus' arms while the real tough guy turned to Jesus, knocking him in the eye. Then Jesus grabbed hold of the bully's jacket to prevent another blow and whirled him around. The fighter went flying in another direction as Jesus put his foot up to his butt but quickly regained his balance. He came after Jesus again. It was like stopping a bull. Jesus tried to hold him back but the bully was too quick for Jesus and was aiming a fist intending to knock Jesus to the ground again.

One hard shove knocked Jesus to the ground. Seeing the young man coming after him, Jesus quickly lifted his arms to protect his face while at the same time pushing the brute away. Jesus' hand suddenly turned yellowish red and then a burst of power shot out from his hand and the bad guy was knocked down.

There was silence for a few moments. The two other bad guys released their hold on Lazarus and took a few steps back shocked at what they had just seen.

Lazarus approached Jesus and they both stared at the bully now laying on the ground. In fact, Lazarus too was very surprised, he was the first to speak, "How-how-did- you- do that?"

Jesus couldn't take his eyes off the bully. He was just lying there with a surprised look on his face.

Pulling on Jesus' arm, Lazarus cried, "Come on, let's get out of here!"

Jesus did not budge.

"Come on, let's go"

10

The bully lay there, not moving.

Jesus walked over to the body. Then bent down kneeling by this teen's side.

Lazarus motioned for Jesus to get out of there before all the festival people arrived back and blamed him for killing this young man.

The other two bandits turned tail and ran.

At this point, Jesus laid a hand upon the man's heart and just as quickly it came back to life. Slowly his eyes began to flutter then shut then flutter again and then opened.

Surprised Lazarus said, "He's alive?"

Jesus nodded.

"Let's get out of here before he gets to his feet. If he was angry before he'll surely be angry, NOW."

As Jesus started to get up, a hand caught his wrist. It was the teen. He pulled Jesus close to his face and he heard in a very soft voice utter the words, "Thanks."

A few moments later he struggled to get up to his feet, and with the help from Jesus, he did it. Arm over Jesus' shoulders and Lazarus too, the young man managed to get to a nearby shade tree and the three teens sat. Water on a close by stand provided water for the young victim. They all drank and it helped with the sun's heat.

Feeling better the boy spoke sounding stronger. "You sure did knock me for a loop when you did that...power thing, on me." The boy said, "You got to tell me how you did that."

"I . . . I don't know."

"Oh, sure you do."

"I'm sorry I really have no idea…"

"Can you help me to the nearest outhouse? I got to go bad."

On the way to the outhouse, the bully turned the other cheek and said, "Look, I'm Prince Rau, I will reward you handsomely."

"It's okay you keep your coins, I really and truly have no idea how that happened. In fact, that was the first time that has ever happened to me."

"Okay, keep it a secret."

While Prince Rau was in the outhouse, Lazarus reached over and spoke in Jesus' ear, "I hope that when I die, you will be around to bring me back to life."

Jesus just gave his friend a smile.

When he came from the outhouse, he was still amazed at what had happened to him.

"How did you do that? No one has ever done that to me before. No one! I don't think anyone has ever done it to my father's army, either. Do you know how valuable something like that would be in our army? Something like that could help our country win wars."

"Wars! Why does there have to be any wars? God has given humans anything they desire," Jesus said.

"Oh, don't be silly. Don't you realize it's gold that gives humans that power?"

Jesus spoke up, "And when that gold runs out what do you have? Land that has been destroyed and not good for anyone."

"You got that wrong. Think of all those poor people out there who need guidance. The rich, like my father, provide that. And it takes war for them to understand. The poor always gives to the rich, so they have very little of their own." Prince Rau said. "That's the law of society. You mention the word god, God. God is a religion..."

Prince Rau thought for a moment then continued, "And therefore wars are caused by religion?"

"That's true. Man-made religion causes wars. God hates organized religion. If I were him, I would never preach in a building. I would preach in meadows or street corners. Once a man is trapped in a building, he is seduced by a regular preacher not called by God. They are easily misled by all the finery they see around them. Just because a man can speak doesn't mean he speaks from his heart. Most false preachers speak from their pocketbooks." Jesus continued, "God wants everyone on Earth to love one another. Cause when you love, you have respect for one another, if you have respect for one another, you won't want to harm them in any way. It's in the commandments." Jesus noticed Prince Rau's face was turning red. Then he said in a friendly voice, "Calm yourself."

"Well, you can think what you will but my father has many soldiers at his command. And he would like nothing more than to eliminate all Christians off the face of the earth." The prince said.

Jesus, bit his tongue, for the moment, knowing when not to press the issue any further.

Prince Rau needed to cool off when Lazarus spoke, "Anyone for a swim?"

Jesus replied, "Hey that would be fun."

Prince Rau said, "Aum, I-I don't know how to."

Lazarus, "It's nothing, all you do is jump in."

Jesus spoke, "There's a little more to it than just jumping in. Come on. I heard princes aren't afraid of anything."

Regaining his composer said, the prince said, "Okay, let's go."

Jesus asked before they left, "Where are your two friends?"

"There probably on the other side of the world by now. There a bunch of chickens, you know."

With that comment, all three had a good laugh.

The three teens headed to a water hole that; Jesus and Lazarus knew about. Two of them hung their robes on nearby bushes and jumped in. Jesus was a good swimmer and Lazarus was even better.

"Hey, Jesus," Lazarus called. "Do that trick again. You know," his fingers walked on top of the water.

"No, Lazarus," came a firm tone from his friend.

There were a few other boys in the swimming hole as well. They would not be alone. A swimming hole is the best place to cool off from the hot sun.

The sun rose high over their heads and in the afternoon several other boys came up over the hill and headed toward the swimming hole. They dropped their robes and now were completely naked.

All of them jumping in at the same time made a big splash.

The rest of the afternoon was spent splashing each other along with laughing and playing funny tricks. Sometimes the bolder ones would slip under the water and yank the loincloth off another boy and watch as his face turn red with embarrassment.

Both Jesus and Lazarus looked around for their newfound friend and saw him still standing on the bank. Jesus swam to the bank and looked up and asked him, "Aren't you going to come in?"

"At home, my servants always undress me." Prince Rau said in a dignified manner.

"But your servants are not here."

"I will wait for them to arrive. I have no problem waiting."

Jesus thought about it for a moment.

"Come on in, Rau. The water is fine." Lazarus yelled out.

A cold look came from the prince, as he said, "Prince Rau. If you please."

The fact he didn't want to go in is that this bully was very shy to reveal his body to any strangers.

Jesus then got up out of the water and climbed up on the bank and stood next to the prince. "Your royal highness, may I be your humble servant?"

"Yes, you may."

Jesus removed the royal cloak the prince was wearing. Folded it nicely. And placed it gently in the weeds. The prince stood there waiting for the rest of his clothes to be removed. Suddenly Jesus gave him a very heavy push and Prince Rau was in the water splashing about.

Jesus mumbled, "I owed you that." Then Jesus jumped back into the water.

The rest of the afternoon was spent in splashing and laughing.

"The sunset looks so artistic," one of the boys commented.

But each boy knew it was time to go home.

Jesus replied, "Yes, it is. This whole world is just as, you say, artistic. It has forests, desserts, oceans, and mountains, not to mention valleys, if you destroy all that you have nothing but an ugly sight."

"How do you know? Do you travel?" the prince asked.

"Surely you don't think this is the only place on Earth there is?"

"My dad says it is."

"A man who closes his mind to his surroundings and knows only the area for which he has never travelled will never know what lies beyond his door. Therefore, judges the world only by what he sees."

"But how can you be so sure?"

Jesus just smiled at him and handed him his robe.

11

"Jesus before I return home, I want to ask you something. I saw you speaking to a lot of those boys who were swimming, in their own language. How is it you know so many tongues?"

"I have lived in this area for 17 years. There are people who come to the places I've been and they bring their native tongues with them.

Look around you, who swam with us today? Nazarenes, Hebrews, Gentiles, Philistines. They all speak a different language yet these are young folks who see the world with love; they haven't been taught to hate. Until people like kings who rule with an iron fist come along and destroy their world.

Their parents had to come from other places other than just here. So, there must be other lands, other cultures other things to see. It's not just us who live in this valley. There's more to this world than you and I."

"What you say is true. I hadn't thought of that. Come to think of it, there wasn't a bad child among them today. You know, your awfully smart for someone who is 16 years."

"17," he corrected. Jesus just smiled at the compliment.

The prince got to thinking, "Even the ones I was hanging around with at the festival were only there because I order them there. They had no respect for me other than that I am a prince. They were there because I put fear into them."

"You can change and be a good guy."

"I'm good now."

"I didn't say you weren't, good. But we can always better ourselves."

"Well," The prince said. "Here's where I depart with you. My home is down this trail first castle to the right. See ya friend."

"See you, Prince Rauuuuuu."

"What was that?"

"Just a nickname I gave you."

He laughed, "Mine for you is going to be Pushy."

"Why?"

"No one has ever dared push a prince in the water until you came along,"

They both laughed as they departed their way back home.

By now Jesus was growing up. He was 18 years of age.

Handsome as the devil, he was. Jesus became an ace carpenter. His good friends, Lazarus and Prince Rau still hung around with him, even though they too were getting older. You could tell because all three were sporting a beard just as their forefathers had done before them.

The boys had many girlfriends and just as many heartbreaks.

The places they used to go to had different interests now. The tree house, for instance, was all rotted away and forgotten about. The time for play was much less than it used to be. More adult statuses took over in their minds.

By now, they had to concentrate on things like responsibility. They had to look and plan for the future, plan to get a wife and then plan on having children with wives.

One early morning, Prince Rau, rode up to the house of Joseph where Jesus was still living.

"Hey, pushy," He called from his horse.

Jesus came to the door. "What do you want so early?"

"Do you want to go exploring? I know where there is a cave."

"Sure, RAAA-u-u-u-u-u." By now they had nicknames for one another. "As soon as I get this leg on this table. Want some breakfast?"

"Sure, I do." He came in and sat at a table and helped himself to some bread." Mary was out fetching more water.

"Hey, pushy, look I now served myself." He said that with pride.

"You're improving. Keep up the good work."

By now Jesus didn't need to ask his father to leave the shop. His father always had been down to earth and trusted him. After all, he does have a beard now.

When the prince was done, he said, "Let's go pick up Lazy."

Jesus jumped on their mule and proceeded to follow Prince Rau to Lazarus' house. He was in the back picking vegetables from their garden.

"You want to go exploring?" The prince shouted.

"Sounds like fun and adventurous."

Before long all three set out to locate the cave.

The horse and mule stepped carefully over loose stones. They knew one slip; would be fatal. The ride was bumpy and harsh but being teens, they were used to their spines being jolted. Many times, they would have to duck low from hanging branches. Hill after hill, up and over trails and besides it was getting hot.

Finally, the three came to a little valley. It seemed it had been cleared out and they noticed many cut branches were laying against the hillside.

"Why?"

"That's odd," Lazarus said.

"Clearly someone is hiding something," Prince Rau noticed. "Why had all those branches been cut down? Let's check it out."

Now when you are young, you don't take into account the danger you can get into because it's a challenge to see who will chicken out first.

The teens got off their horses and mules and approached the branches with caution.

"Hmmmmmm, I feel a cool breeze coming from the other side of those limbs," Jesus said.

One by one they removed branches from the entrance of a cave. It was the one they had been searching for.

Looking into the cave, darkness was all they could see.

"I know, we'll make a torch from these branches we removed." Gathering the branches and then tying them together formed a huge unlit torch.

"Anyone bring a lighting flint?"

Jesus said he brought one from home.

"That's good. Strike it and let the sparks catch the leaves on fire." Lazarus told.

After several clicks of the flint, a few sparks flew onto one of the dead leaf's settings it ablaze. Soon it was providing light in the dark cave.

The blaze was so hot and bright they had to be careful of it.

Stone walls, lined the wall of the hollowed tunnel as the boys continued to follow its trail inward. They felt coolness on their legs. The boys continued.

Those teens inched their way through the cavern not knowing what to expect. Step by step the rocks became sharper and many times they stepped into a hole, ankle-deep, and fell forward. Sometimes all three would end up scraping their knees from falls.

Lazarus was walking clinging to the walls of the cave when something sharp scraped his toe. Reaching down picked it up, to find it was an old spear with a stone arrowhead tied to a pole which was broken in half.

"Look! See what I found."

Holding the light from the torch to it found it was a spear dropped by a soldier. Lazarus wonder why it had been broken in two.

Prince Rau said, more in a whisper, "He may have been fighting off something big down here."

"Like what?"

There was a long pause then in another whisper, "I – I – don't know."

Lazarus, a little concerned and a little scared, said, "I'm ready to leave. How about you?"

Prince Rau snapped; "Are you a scaredy-baby?"

Lazarus defending himself said; "N-no." Then finding an excuse to get out of the cave replied, "The fire is almost out. We'll be in the dark."

Prince Rau, "Perhaps you're right. We should be heading back."

As the three turned to head back, a tiny squeak was heard near the ceiling of the cave, followed but many more squeaks that seemed to be getting louder and then the sound of rushing wings.

Prince Rau yelled out, "Bats! BATS! LET'S GET OUT OF HERE!"

They ran toward the entrance of the cave as the bats flew above their heads. As they reached outside Jesus raised his hand against the flying beasts, but nothing happened. Jesus was confused.

By now, stars were starting to come out and the sky was a nice shade of purple.

The young men laughed and rolled in the grass with so much laughter. But they knew the time had come for all of them to head back home.

They mounted their four-footed transportation and headed home. When they reached a fork in the road, they bid their goodbyes to each other. Lazarus left by the road west. The young men watched him disappear into the darkness.

Soon they came to another fork and the rider Prince Rau plopped eastward and he too disappeared into hills. Jesus was the only one left to travel back home alone.

12

Mary loved her son very much and lived near him although there were times when Jesus had to remind her that he was going about his father's business. Sometimes, she didn't understand her son but knew there was nothing she could do about it. She knew he had a mission to do.

His brothers and sisters went their separate ways. One became a jester in the king's court and another mended clothing. James became an advisor to the king, while another became a stable hand. Each brother or sister became somewhat successful. While Jesus became a good teacher and taught not in a church but in the fields out in the open.

Lazarus always remained friends with Jesus even through his adult life. By the way, he never did find out how Jesus did those special tricks.

Prince Rau didn't have too many years left to be friends because he died on his 23rd birthday. It was sad, they were good friends all three of them.

Jesus always was close to his father. In fact, in the final days of Joseph's existence, they sat on a hill looking at the evening sky just talking of old times.

By now Jesus was 28 and he was thinking of the death of Prince Rau. He got to talking to his father saying; "People on this planet live a very short time."

"Yes, son they do."

"So then, why can't people learn to love one another? Knowing their time is like a vapour?"

"This I cannot tell you, son. Only God knows, but then again, I wonder if even he has that answer."

"It's funny with Prince Rau. He was such a bully when I first met him. Yet when he passed, he was a kind individual, liked by many."

"I do know, that you are going to become a great teacher...perhaps of all time. You, son, are here for a reason. To teach the truth and fight the war of hatred. It will be hard. I do believe you will be a great servant, a leader of men."

".... but-I'm scared."

"May I make a suggestion?"

"Sure."

"Go out there and gather yourself some strong followers. Teach them the ways of God. But you know something. You are the son of God. And he has given you wisdom, even more than any wise man or king on this planet. You have been with God and it is He who chose you. Do you think for one minute he would let you down? I don't think so."

"I...I, yeah your right."

"Remember the time, Prince Rau bullied you and you hit him with some sort of power?"

"Yes. I never could figure out what happened that day."

"That was the power of the holy ghost coming from within you. God loves his son and like any father would give his son things to defend himself in times of need. You have all the angels in heaven who would fight for you if you give a command to do so, like that Powerball."

"Why didn't it work on those bats?"

"Those bats are animals and you were in their territory. It was them that needed protection, not you."

"Oh, now I understand what that gift of myrrh was for, that the wise men gave me."

"It's to tell you that someday you will die," Joseph held his son close to him. "The myrrh stands for hope and the healing power of the people."

Tears were running down Joseph's face, but he quickly regained his composure. "WOW! The holy ghost just spoke to me in a daydream and it's not even night yet. He told me to tell you to have no fear of the future." Joseph told Jesus with a smile.

"Even thou you are my stepdad; I love you very much."

"And I love you as well."

"I am so proud of you and couldn't as for a better son than you."

Joseph died a few months later. It was a sad day for the Christ family.

A few years later, Jesus was about 30 and one of his sisters was getting married. During her wedding reception, she ran out of wine. Not knowing what to do about it, ran and told Mary.

That's when Mary called out "JESUS!"

IT IS HERE I WILL LEAVE YOU BECAUSE I TOLD YOU IN THIS TALE WHAT IT MAY HAVE BEEN LIKE FOR JESUS AS A CHILD. NOW I TURN YOU OVER TO THE TRUE AUTHORS OF HIS LIFE BEGINNING AT AGE 30.

So, what happened? I can't tell you that, it's like a cliffhanger. If you want to know, then turn and read a book called The Bible. It will tell you the rest of the story of Jesus as an adult. I just told you in fiction about his life as a boy.

I want to give a special thanks to those who aided me in this book.

My wife Cova Jean Brown

Who so many times erased my pencil markings off my illustrations, sharpened my pencils and organized my table so I could work.

My Publisher Mahip Bhatia

Who has published many of my books and made me go further than I thought I could. He has published not only mine but others' so give him a chance to get your book published.

Jose Galvez

Aided me in doing research.

Apple Computer Team

Corrected many of my mistakes. If they hadn't gone to school of technology I'd be using a typewriter and several bottles of whiteout.

Susan Brown, Kelly Brown, and Dinesh Saini

Came to my rescue many times when I had trouble figuring things out on this contraption.

THE END

OR IS IT THE BEGINNING?

www.ingramcontent.com/pod-product-compliance
Lightning Source LLC
Chambersburg PA
CBHW021011180726
47993CB00019B/2322